Scary Stories to Tell if You D
Collected from folklore and retold by Joe Oliveto
Illustration designs by Joe Oliveto
Copyright © 2017 by Joe Oliveto
All Rights Reserved

Table of Contents

IN THE DARK

Growing up, my favorite book was *Scary Stories to Tell in the Dark.* My favorite TV show was *The Twilight Zone*. Before my age was in the double digits, I had seen *Halloween, The Exorcist, Psycho, Night of the Living Dead,* and many others.

As an adult, little has changed. Whenever I'm with friends, I wait for someone to start talking about something scary that happened to them.

For some people, fear is fun. There's something exciting about hearing a ghost story. When the story is good enough, you can believe anything is real.

But it's not just about fear. Scary stories give us the chance to learn about the culture of a time and a place. We hear them, and we learn what scared people in the past, what scares them now, and—if we pay attention—we even learn why.

This book is a passion project, a tribute *Scary Stories to Tell in the Dark* and the many other creepy tales for kids that we read in our childhood. It has no official relationship with that series, or with any of its publishers. But hopefully, it manages to capture the spirit of the originals.

Don't just read these stories to yourself. Share them with friends. Tell them around the campfire. Tell your own versions. They're meant to be shared.

Because, I'm sure for many of you, and for many of your friends, fear really is fun. It always has been for me.

Joe Oliveto

OTHER WORLDS

Most people don't think these types of stories could ever be real. But others aren't so sure...

FOLLOWED HOME

Kate was walking home alone one night. She had to go down a dark country road to get there. Besides Kate, there was no one on the road. As she walked, she began to imagine seeing ghosts and monsters hiding in the shadows.

"Don't be silly," Kate told herself. "There's nothing scary about this road in the daytime. So there's nothing to be scared of now either."

But soon after, Kate thought she heard footsteps behind her. She turned around and saw a small boy following behind her. He walked slowly. It was too dark to see his face.

Kate waved hello, but the boy didn't wave back. She decided to keep walking. A little boy couldn't hurt her.

As she walked, the boy's footsteps got louder and louder. Kate looked over her shoulder again. Instead of a little boy, now it looked like a teenager was following her. Even though he was still walking slowly, he seemed a lot closer.

"Your mind is playing tricks on you," Kate said to herself. "It's just dark out. You thought you saw a little boy because he was far away."

Still, Kate decided to start walking faster. She wanted to run, but for some reason she thought the person behind her would run after her if she did.

No matter how fast Kate walked, his footsteps kept getting closer. She looked back again. This time, the figure was heavier. She still couldn't see its face, but it wasn't a teenager anymore. Now it was a grown man.

Kate wanted to believe she was just imagining things. But she wasn't so sure.

"Can I help you?" Kate asked. Maybe the man was lost. Maybe he just needed to ask her for directions.

The man didn't answer. He kept walking, slowly getting closer.

Kate turned back. Now she could see her house at the end of the road. She started to run, but the man's footsteps still sounded closer and closer.

When she reached her driveway, Kate spun around once more to look at the man following her.

He was an old man now, and he was very, very close. For the first time, she could see his face. He was so thin he almost looked like a skeleton. The old man glared at Kate with anger in his eyes.

Kate dashed inside and locked the door behind her. She was so loud her parents came rushing to find out what was wrong.

"There's a man following me!" Kate said.

Her parents searched for almost an hour, but they couldn't find any trace of him.

VANISHED

Ben and his parents lived in a big farmhouse out in the country. One cold morning, he woke up early to get some wood for the fire. After a few minutes passed, his mother called him in for breakfast.

Ben didn't reply, though. His mother tried again. He still didn't reply.

His mother and father were worried. They went outside to look for Ben, but they couldn't find him. They called his name again and again, but he never answered. After a little while, they called the police to come help.

Everyone wondered if Ben was kidnapped. For days, people from all over helped look for him. They searched through the woods and all around the farm, hoping to find him. No one found anything, though. Pretty soon, everyone but the police and Ben's parents gave up.

One night, about a week later, Ben's mother was trying to sleep, when she heard Ben's voice cry out for her.

"Mom," he seemed to say, "Where are you?"

The voice was coming from somewhere outside. She rushed out to where she thought she heard it, but no one was there.

Then, she heard the voice again. "Mom," it said, "I can't find you."

"I'm right here, Ben!" his mother said. "I'm right here."

But she still couldn't see him. She and her husband searched to find where the voice was coming from, but no matter how clear it sounded, they couldn't find Ben. They looked for hours, but there was no sign of him.

That happened every night for almost a month. Ben's mother and father would hear him calling for them. They would search the farm for hours, but they never found anything. Each night, Ben's voice sounded more and more distant.

Then, one day, it stopped. No one knew what happened, and no one ever heard or saw Ben ever again.

THE SHADOW MAN

Jake and his family had moved into the old farmhouse by the woods. That's when the bad dreams started. Except they weren't dreams. His parents said they were, but Jake knew better.

The first night in his new home, Jake woke up after his parents had gone to sleep. He tried to move, but he couldn't. No matter how hard he tried, he just couldn't move an inch.

That's when he saw the man in his doorway. He was the same size and shape as a man, but instead of clothes or hair or a face, he was just a dark figure, like a shadow.

Jake tried to call for help, but no sounds would come out of his mouth.

The shadow man slowly walked into the room. The closer he got, the more Jake tried to scream, but he still couldn't. All he could do was watch the shadow get closer and closer.

Finally, the shadow man was next to him. It was just a dark figure, but it wasn't flat like a shadow is. It was like there was an empty blank space where a person should be.

The shadow looked at him for a few moments. Jake couldn't even close his eyes.

Suddenly, it disappeared. As soon as it did, Jake was able to move and talk again. He ran into his parents' room and told them what happened.

Jake's father searched the house. He couldn't find anyone.

Every single night, the same thing happened. Jake couldn't explain why, but he felt like the shadow man wanted to hurt him.

At first, his parents said he was having nightmares. They said he was just getting used to living in a new place. But after a week, Jake's mom decided to bring him to a doctor.

The doctor said Jake's mind was just playing tricks on him. He told Jake and his mom that sometimes people wake up and see things like that. It happened to a lot of people. The doctor said it would soon go away on its own.

But it didn't. One night, Jake asked if he could have a friend sleep over. He thought he'd be less afraid if he wasn't alone. Jake didn't tell his friend about the shadow man, though. He didn't want him to laugh.

They stayed up late telling stories and playing games. Jake hated going to sleep now. He always tried to stay awake as long as possible. After a while, though, his friend started to get tired. They feel asleep soon.

Again, Jake woke up in the middle of the night. Like every other night, he watched as the shadow man walked into the room and up to his bed. As always, he couldn't move.

But this time, the shadow man didn't get all the way to his bed. It disappeared when Jake's friend woke up screaming.

Jake's parents rushed in to find out what was wrong.

"There was a man standing by Jake's bed!" his friend said. "But it wasn't really a man. It was just a shadow."

THE NEW WIFE

Once there was a man who fell in love with a pretty young girl who moved into town. He wanted to marry her, but he couldn't. He already had a wife of his own.

The man couldn't forget about the pretty girl though. They would go on long walks together when his wife thought he was staying late at work.

He decided he would poison his wife. With her dead, he could marry his new love.

The man cooked a big dinner one night. He pretended it was a special gift for his wife. She didn't know he had poisoned her drink.

Soon after taking a sip, she began to choke. The man watched her, doing nothing to help. As she took her last breath, his wife looked at him with a face of pure anger. Just before she died, she realized what her husband had done.

The man hid the body in the woods and told everyone his wife was missing. After a long time, everyone assumed she had died. He was free to marry his new bride.

But everywhere the man went, he thought he saw his old wife. Sometimes he would spot her on a crowded street, staring at him with the same face she made when she died. Sometimes he'd look in the mirror and see her standing behind him, but when he turned around, no one was there. Every night, he had nightmares about her.

None of that worried him. He told himself he was just imagining things. Nothing was going to stop him from marrying the pretty young girl.

The day of his wedding finally arrived. His bride had chosen the most beautiful dress he had ever seen. When the wedding ceremony was complete, the man lifted his bride's veil to kiss her.

The woman he saw wasn't his pretty young wife. Instead, he saw the angry face of his old wife.

In shock, he grabbed her by the throat and tried to strangle her. Before he could kill her once more, people in the crowd pulled him away.

They helped the bride to her feet. Suddenly, she didn't look like his old wife anymore. Now she was the pretty young girl again.

But everyone had seen the man try to kill her. He spent the rest of his life in prison.

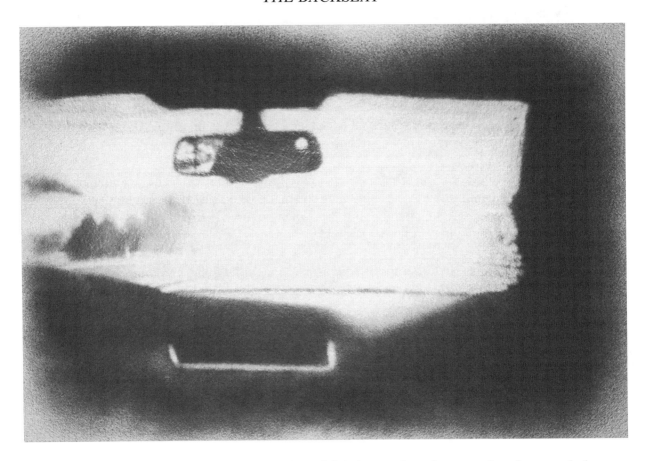

Jenny and Eddie had just gotten married. They didn't have a lot of money, but they needed a car. One day when they were out shopping they found exactly the one they wanted. It was an old classic, just the kind they liked.

A car like that should have cost a lot more than they could afford. But when they asked the man who owned the shop how much it cost, the price was much lower than they expected.

"We'll buy it," Jenny said.

"Okay," the shop owner said. "But everyone who buys that car always brings it back."

Jenny and Eddie couldn't imagine why anyone would bring back such a perfect car. They didn't think much about it. They were just happy they found their dream car at such a great price.

For the first few weeks, Jenny and Eddie used it to go on long drives all across the state. Even when they had nowhere they needed to go, they just liked driving it.

But when either one of them drive it alone, it was different. Both noticed a weird smell anytime they drove it alone.

"It's an old car," Eddie said. "Sometimes old cars smell funny."

They tried not to let it bother them, but things got worse. Soon, Jenny started to feel like there was someone watching her from the backseat when she was driving. When she turned around there was no one there.

Then one day, she got that feeling and looked in the rearview mirror.

Looking back at her, she saw two mean, ugly eyes. They looked like the eyes of a killer.

She quickly looked back, but again, there was no one there.

Jenny and Eddie decided they'd had enough. They brought the car back to the shop and told the dealer about what happened.

That's when he told them the truth. "There's a reason people keep bring this car back," he said. "It used to belong to a famous gangster. Someone shot him in it years ago. Now everyone says it's haunted."

THE DARE

Kevin and Tony were friends. There was an old mansion on their street that no one lived in anymore. Everyone said it was haunted. Some of the older kids even said they had seen the ghost of an old woman sitting in a rocking chair by the attic window once.

One day Kevin dared Tony to break into it. Tony didn't want to. His parents had told him not to go near that house. But he knew Kevin would make fun of him if he didn't.

"Go up to the attic when you get inside," Kevin said. Don't just wait by the front door."

"Okay," Tony said.

"Take a picture when you get up there to prove it."

Tony said he would.

It was easy to break into the house. The front door was unlocked. Kevin stood behind and watched Tony go inside.

Fifteen minutes passed. Then a half hour. Then an hour.

Kevin walked up to the house and shouted for Tony, but he didn't get an answer. He was too afraid to go inside and check for Tony.

Instead, he went home and told his parents what happened. They called the police. An officer searched the old house and found Tony in the attic. He was dead. The doctor couldn't figure out how he died. The only clue they had was picture Tony took in the attic.

There was an old woman in the picture, sitting in a rocking chair by the window.

THE BLACK DOG

John Brent lived with his family in a big house near town. One night he couldn't sleep, so he went over to the window to look out at the yard.

As he looked outside, he spotted something looking at him. He squinted to see what it was.

In the yard was a big, black dog. John had never seen it before. It didn't move or make a sound. It just sat in the yard, looking up at him.

John stared at the dog for a few moments. He was a grown man, but some reason, this dog scared him. Usually he would have gone outside and chased it away, but something was different tonight. After some time, he went back to bed. When he woke up, the dog was gone.

John became very sick soon after that. His family spent a lot of money for him to see the best doctors around, but he kept getting worse. During this time, he saw the dog in all sorts of places. Sometimes it was sitting by the side of the road when he drove to see one of his doctors. Other times it would follow John as he walked to town.

No one else ever saw it until the night John died. His family stood around his hospital bed when they noticed a look of terror on his face. They turned to see what he was looking at.

It was the big black dog. No one could figure out how it got all the way up to the hospital room.

They chased after it, but the dog ran away. They looked down the halls, but no one could find it. Soon, they decided to go back to John's room.

When they got there, he was dead.

THE HAUNTED TREASURE

Everyone knew about the treasure. Years ago, a pirate buried it somewhere in the county. But no one knew the exact spot.

One night, an old woman had a dream. In it, she saw that the treasure was buried between the roots of a big tree in a nearby field. At first, she didn't think much of the dream. But the next night, she had the dream again. And the night after that. Each time, there was more and more detail.

She told her two grandsons about the dream. They said they would go out to find the treasure. Then they would all be rich.

"Be careful," the old woman warned. "You must be completely silent when you dig. The pirate killed one of his crew and buried him with the treasure so his ghost would guard it. If you say a single word, you'll wake him."

The grandsons promised they would be completely quiet.

When they got to the tree, it was very dark out. They went late at night, so no one would see what they were doing. Everyone in town wanted to find that treasure. They didn't want anyone else to know where it was.

For an hour, one grandson dug a big hole between the roots of the tree, while the other stood guard. Then they switched.

The other grandson dug for about half an hour, when his shovel hit something solid. He leaned in to take a closer look.

"It's the treasure chest!" he said, turning to his brother. "We're rich!"

But his brother didn't look happy. His brother looked scared. When he turned back around, he saw why.

Standing in front of him was a tall man with anger in his eyes. He wore old pirate clothes, and had a scar across his neck. He ran towards the two brothers, reaching out to grab them.

They both sprinted away, running through the field as fast as they could. When they got home, they told the old woman what had happened. They described the terrible man who had chased them.

"You forgot my warning," she said. "That was the ghost from my dream."

The next morning, they headed back to the field. When they got there, the big hole they had dug the night before was completely filled in, as if they had never been there.

Somehow, word got out about their story, and people in town talked about it for years. A long time later, some other young men heard it one night from an uncle. They drove off to find the treasure. When morning came, people found their car parked in the field near the tree. But no one ever saw those young men again.

Ellen lived down the road from the old hospital. It had closed down before she was born, but everyone said they used to lock up crazy people there. Some of them were even killers. A lot of people thought the place was haunted, but Ellen didn't believe in those sorts of things.

One night, she was having a sleepover with three other girls. They all started telling scary stories about the hospital. The other girls said that the ghosts of the people who used to live there still roamed the halls.

"That's dumb," Ellen said. "Ghosts aren't real."

"Oh yeah?" another girl said. "If you're so brave, why don't you spend an hour in there?"

"Fine," Ellen said. "There's nothing to be afraid of."

The girls headed out to the hospital. It was dark and shadowy. Near the front, they found an open doorway where they could sneak in. One of the girls pointed a flashlight inside. There was a hallway, with a small room at the end of it.

"That's the room where they kept the really bad people," she said. "Ellen, you go in there and close the door behind you. We'll wait out here for you. If you stay there for an hour, we'll know you're as brave as you say."

Ellen went down the hallway, into the small room. She closed the door. The other girls waited. Soon, they thought they heard the sound of Ellen screaming, and someone banging on the door.

"I hope she's okay," one of the girls said.

"She is," another said. "She's just playing a trick on us."

The screaming and banging didn't stop, though. Soon, the youngest girl got really worried.

"We should go check on her," she said. "Just to make sure."

They headed towards the room. Even with the flashlight, they could barely see. When they got in front of the door, the sounds stopped.

The youngest girl opened the door and pointed the flashlight in. Ellen was nowhere to be found.

"She's just trying to fool us," the oldest girl said. "She probably snuck out of the room and is hiding somewhere."

They searched and searched. They called out Ellen's name. But she never answered back, and they never saw her again.

MILK BOTTLES

Many years ago, an old man ran a shop in town. One day, a pale young woman walked in.

"Can I help you?" he asked.

The woman didn't say anything, but she pointed at a bottle of milk. The old man sold it to her. She walked out without saying a word.

The next day, she came to the shop again. When the shopkeeper asked her what she wanted that day, she pointed to a bottle of milk, like the day before. She still didn't speak a word.

The same thing happened the next day. Later that night, the old man told some of his friends in town about the strange young woman. So when she went to the shop again the next day, some of them followed her to see where she went after she left.

They followed her through town, but she walked very fast and they couldn't keep up with her. The men saw her walk up a hill and into the graveyard. She stopped by a grave by a tree. Then they lost sight of her.

The men found the grave it looked like she had stopped at. It belonged to a woman and her new baby who had both gotten sick and died just a few days earlier. They wanted to know more about the woman, so they got a few other people from town and dug up the coffin. When they started to lift it, they thought they heard a crying sound coming from inside.

The townspeople opened the coffin. In it was the body of the young woman. Her baby was in her arms.

But the baby was still alive. It looked weak and small, but it was alive.

Beside the baby and its mother were four empty milk bottles.

DANGERS

These stories may not be true, but they feel like they could be...

THE PICTURE

Laura took great pictures. She always had her camera with her, taking photos of her friends, family, and pets. But it never bothered anyone. Her work was so good that some people would even pay her to take pictures of them.

Her favorite thing to photograph, though, was the woods. She loved the trees, and the rocks, and the streams. If the weather was nice, sometimes she'd camp out there for the weekend. When she came back, she knew she'd have hundreds of photos to look at. Sometimes she would bring a friend along. But not always.

That weekend, she woke up early and headed straight to the woods. She wanted to get a nice picture of the sunrise. After that, she decided she'd spend the rest of the day getting as many pictures of the trees as she could. Then she would pitch a tent and get some sleep.

It was a very nice day. Laura had packed food, but she was having such a good time that she almost forgot to eat it. When night came, she was surprised at how quickly the day went.

Laura pitched her tent, ate a quick meal, and went to bed. She'd been walking all day, and was tired. She left the camera by the door of the tent. That way, she could grab it and take more sunrise pictures in the morning.

It didn't take long for her to fall asleep.

When she awoke, the sun was already up. So, she packed her things and hurried back to her car. She was excited to get home and look at her pictures.

They were all perfect. The photos of the sunrise looked beautiful. So did the photos of the trees. Laura was very happy with all of them.

Until she saw a picture she didn't take. At first, she wasn't sure what she was looking at. When she realized what it was, a shiver ran down her spine.

The picture was of her, sleeping in the tent.

THE GUEST

The man lived alone in a big house. But for a long time, he hadn't felt like he was alone. He heard strange noises at night, like someone was moving around in the other rooms. Food would often go missing. Sometimes, he'd go into town to do some shopping. When he got back, certain things would be different. Maybe a chair wouldn't be where he left it. Or the curtains would be closed, even though he knew he left them open.

He told people in town about it. A lot of them said his house might be haunted. But he didn't believe in ghosts. Still, he decided to set up video cameras in some of the rooms. When he went out, he would turn them on. If there was a ghost, it would show up on the video.

He hid one camera in the kitchen, one in his bedroom, and one in the living room. Then he left. He stayed in town for hours. By the time he got back, it was night.

The old man took a seat at the kitchen table and started watching the videos. First he watched the video of his bedroom. Then the one from the dining room. There was nothing strange in them. He was starting to get tired, and feeling pretty foolish. "This is silly," he told himself. "I've just been imagining things."

But he decided to watch the kitchen video before going to bed. It would be easier to sleep if he knew there was nothing to be afraid of.

For a few minutes, nothing happened. He was ready to turn the video off, when he noticed something. In the video, one of the big cupboard doors opened. Out of it crawled a skinny woman with stringy black hair. Her face was pale, and her clothes were almost shreds. She took some food out of the pantry and sat at the table to eat it. Then, she crawled back in the cupboard and closed the door behind her.

The old man was frozen with fear. He never checked that big cupboard. He barely ever thought about it. He didn't have a big family to feed, so he didn't keep anything in it.

And he was sitting right next to it.

After a long time, he was able to stand up. He walked out the front door and went straight to the police station. At first they didn't believe him, but they decided to check his house just in case.

When they got there, they found the woman from the video, hiding in the cupboard. They found out she was homeless, and had broken into the old man's house one night when he was away.

The police told the old man she'd been living in his cupboard for almost a year.

Adam was driving down a dark road in the woods. It was late, and he wanted to get home. There was no one on the road but him.

Up ahead, he saw something strange. As he got closer, he realized it was a young man lying on the side of the road. He looked like he might be hurt.

Adam knew he should stop and help. But for some reason, he didn't. Something didn't feel right. Instead, he kept driving. As he drove away, he looked in his rearview mirror. He thought he saw the figures of other people standing behind him, but it was dark. Adam told himself he was imagining things.

He drove almost another five miles before pulling over and stopping. Now he felt like he had been silly before. "That man could be dying," Adam told himself. "I have to go back and see if he's okay."

Adam turned around and drove back to the spot where he saw the man. He wasn't there anymore. Instead, there was another car parked on the side of the road around the same spot.

Adam parked his car and got out. He looked around for the man he had seen or the driver of the parked car, but he couldn't find anyone.

"I think there's a police station at the end of this road," he told himself. "I'll let them know what I saw."

Adam got back his car and drove to the police station. When he got there, he told the officer on duty about the man on the side of the road and the parked car.

The officer looked very serious when Adam finished his story. "Wait right here," he said.

The officer rushed into another room. Adam heard him talking to other police officers over the radio. He couldn't hear what they were talking about, but it sounded important.

After a few minutes, the officer came back in to ask Adam more questions.

"What's all this about?" Adam said.

"You're very lucky, young man. A gang of murderers have been tricking people this way. One of them pretends to be hurt on the side of the road while the others hide in the woods. When someone stops to help, the rest of them jump out of the woods and carry the person away."

THE BAG

Rachel had just learned how to drive. One day, she decided to go to the mall. She spent a few hours shopping, and met up with some friends of hers who worked there. Her parents had bought her a new car for her birthday, and she got them both gifts to thank them.

When she got back to the parking lot, though, one of her tires was flat. She didn't know how to fix it, and looked around to see if there might be someone who could help.

A man saw her from nearby and came over. He was carrying a bag that looked like something a person would keep tools in.

"Can you help me?" Rachel asked.

"What's the problem?" the man asked.

"I have a flat tire. This is a new car. I just got my license."

"Sure, I can help you with that," the man said. He changed the tire and told Rachel everything should be fine now.

"Thank you so much," she said. "Can I give you some money for helping me?"

"No, I don't need any money," the man said. "But I took the bus here. I don't want to wait around for the next one. Could you give me a ride to my house? I don't live far."

Rachel said she could do that. The man put his bag down in the trunk, then headed for the front seat.

Suddenly, Rachel changed her mind. Even though the man helped her, he was still a stranger. She knew better than to give rides to strangers. Before he could get in, she started the car and drove away. When she got home, though, she remembered he left his bag in the trunk. She decided to open it up to see what was inside.

There were only two things in the bag. A long rope, and a sharp knife.

THE MESSAGE

Jane and Ashley shared an apartment. Ashley liked to go out to parties at night, but Jane always had to wake up early for her job. It was usually really late when Ashley got back home. She always tried hard not to wake up Jane.

One night, Ashley went out to see some friends. A few minutes after she left, she realized she forgot her wallet. She decided to go back to the apartment and get it.

The lights were off. She figured Jane was asleep, so she didn't turn them on. As she searched for her wallet, she thought she heard some noise from Jane's bed. It sounded like something rustling around.

"She's probably just tossing and turning in her sleep," Ashley told herself. Jane did that sometimes.

Ashley found her wallet, and went back out. She stayed out for a few hours, dancing and partying. When she got home, she went straight to bed.

The next morning, she woke up to a sight that made her scream in terror.

Jane had been murdered in the night. Above her bed, someone wrote a message in blood: "Aren't you glad you didn't turn on the light?"

THE DATE

Jim and Kelly were on their first date together. They went out to dinner, and then they saw a movie. Afterwards, they decided to go driving around the county.

Soon, they ended up on a dark road through the woods. There weren't any houses around or any other cars on the road.

"Did you know this road is haunted?" Jim said.

"Oh, sure," Kelly said.

"No, it's true," Jim said. "There used to be this crazy man who lived in a shack in the woods. If a person's car broke down, he'd find whoever was in it and chop them up with an axe. If you listen close some nights, you can still hear the people he killed screaming for help."

"That's not true," Kelly said. "Those are just stories everyone tells."

Jim and Kelly decided to talk about something else. Even though neither one wanted to admit it, they were both a little scared. So they started telling jokes about some of the other kids at school. After a little while, they started to feel better. There was nothing to be afraid of.

They'd been having such a nice time that Jim forgot to make sure the car had enough gas. When the tank ran out, he had to pull over to the side of the road.

"Oh, no," Kelly said. "We're in the middle of nowhere out here."

"There's a gas station not too far away," Jim said. "I've got a jug I can fill up. I'll walk there and come back with enough gas to get us out of here."

Kelly didn't think it was a great idea. It would be better to wait for someone else to drive by. Then they could signal to them that they needed help. But the road was deserted. And it was late. Another car might not show up until the morning. "Will you be okay out there by yourself?" she asked.

"Sure," Jim said. "It's only about a mile away. I'll be back soon."

Jim got the jug and headed out. Kelly locked the doors behind him. She sat there and waited for him to come back for a very long time. But he didn't show up.

"Where is he?" she asked herself. She tried not to think about story Jim had told her earlier, about the crazy man. It was hard not to, though. The woods outside her window looked dark and eerie. She pulled her coat over her face and hid down, so no one would see her through the windows.

After what seemed like an hour, she heard a strange noise on the top of the car.

Tap-tap-tap. Tap-tap-tap.

"Jim, is that you?" she asked. But no one answered.

She heard it again. *Tap-tap-tap. Tap-tap-tap.*

"This isn't funny!" she shouted. She hoped he was just trying to scare her. But he still didn't answer.

Finally, she pulled her coat away from her face and sat up. She looked out the windows, but couldn't see anyone.

The noise continued. *Tap-tap-tap. Tap-tap-tap.*

She wanted to go out and see what was making the noise. "Maybe my mind is just playing tricks on me," she told herself.

Kelly opened the door and stepped out onto the road. At first, she didn't see anything. Then she looked above the car.

Jim was hanging from a long rope tied to a tree branch. There was a big, bloody wound on his chest.

When his body swayed in the wind, his shoes gently hit the roof of the car. They made a noise when they did.

Tap-tap-tap. Tap-tap-tap.

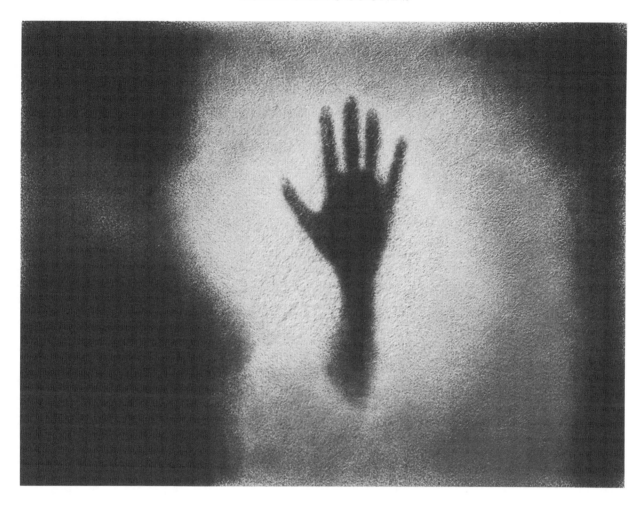

Beth and Anne were college roommates. That night, most of the other students were away. It was almost time for the holiday break, and they had gone home. But Beth and Anne both had a few more tests to take before they could leave.

Usually, the building was filled with other students. Most of the time, it was a lot of fun. But that night, with so many people gone, it was a little scary.

Beth and Anne got along well, though, and told jokes and stories to help each other relax. After that, they decided to watch some TV.

When they turned on the TV, there was a special news report on. An insane killer has escaped from the nearby prison. The report said that anyone living in the area should be extra careful and lock all their doors.

"There's nothing to worry about," Beth said. "That prison isn't really that close. And there's no reason a killer would head this way anyway."

Anne agreed, but they both decided it would be a good idea to lock the door, just in case. They put on a funny TV show, and tried to forget about the whole thing.

A little later, Beth started to feel hungry. She asked Anne if she wanted to go get some food with her.

"No, thanks," Anne said. "I'm getting a little tired. Will you be okay alone?"

"I'll be fine," Beth said. "That killer won't come anywhere near the college. But just to be safe, lock the door behind me. I'll bring my key to let myself back in."

"Okay," Anne said.

An hour passed, and Beth hadn't come back yet. "She probably just saw someone she knew," Anne told herself. "I'm sure she's fine."

Anne was a little worried, but decided to go to sleep. She was sure Beth would be back when she woke up.

But that didn't happen. Instead, Anne awoke in the middle of the night to a strange sound outside her door. Beth was still gone.

It sounded light some sort of animal scratching at the door, trying to get in. Anne sat there in fear. "Go away!" she finally shouted, but whatever was behind the door kept scratching at it.

After what felt like hours, it finally stopped. There was a thudding sound, like something heavy being dropped on the floor. Anne waited for a few moments. When she got up enough courage, she walked slowly to the door and opened it.

Beth was in the hallway, lying in a pool of blood. Someone had stabbed her to death.

But she didn't die right away. Along the door were scratch marks.

And Beth's fingernails were worn down. It looked like she'd been scratching at a door, trying to get in.

Steve and his dad loved camping. Every summer, they would go out into the woods and stay there for a whole weekend.

One time, they found a big stream. The water looked so nice and cool that they decided to take a drink from it. But when Steve tried to drink the water, he felt like there were pebbles in it. He decided not to have any more.

A few weeks later, Steve started to have stomach pains. At first, they weren't that bad, but soon it hurt so much that he couldn't go to school.

His doctor knew there was something wrong. He told Steve's parents to take him in for an X-ray. That way, they could see if there was something in his stomach making him feel so sick.

When they looked at the X-ray, the doctors saw something strange in his stomach. It looked almost like some sort of string or ribbon. They told his parents he would need to have an operation so they could take it out.

Steve went in for the operation. When the doctors took the strange object out of his stomach, everyone shrieked in terror.

It was a live snake. It turned out that the pebbles in Steve's's water from the camping trip weren't pebbles at all. They were snake eggs.

One had hatched in his stomach.

THE ELEVATOR

Sandra lived in the city. One night she got back to her apartment building very late. She lived on the fifth floor.

As she stepped into the elevator, a man rushed behind her, shouting, "Wait, hold the elevator please!"

She held the door open until the man got in. He thanked her and pressed the button for the fourth floor.

Sandra didn't know him, but there were a lot of people in the building she never met. He looked like a nice person. They talked for a few moments as the elevator made its way to the top of the building.

At the fourth floor, the man got out. "Have a nice night," Sandra said.

The man turned back to look at her. "I'll see you on the fifth floor," he said.

At first, Sandra didn't know what he meant. Then she saw it.

The man was holding a sharp, bloody knife. He grinned at her like a crazy person, then darted to the stairs as the elevator doors closed.

Sandra didn't have time to run. The doors closed in front of her. Her building was old and there was no button to stop the elevator.

It started moving up to the fifth floor.

THE TRUCK

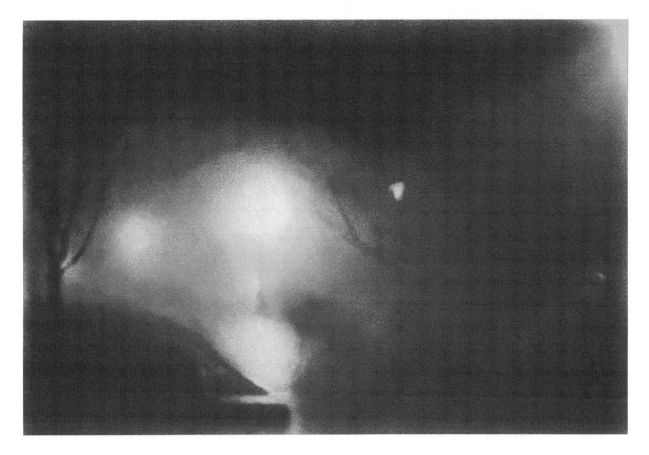

Frank and Donna were married. Some nights, they liked to go out to the country to drive. One night, they ended up on a dark road they had never been on before.

The road was in the middle of the woods. It was long, winding, and narrow. Tall trees rose up on both sides of it. Their branches were so long you almost couldn't see the sky.

Frank and Donna drove for a long time without seeing any cars or houses. Then, Frank noticed a pair of headlights behind them. Even though it was dark, as they got closer, Frank could see that they belonged to an old pickup truck.

"I've never seen a truck that old before," Donna said.

Frank agreed. "I'm surprised it stills runs."

As they drove on, they noticed the truck was speeding up quickly. Soon, it was right behind them. Its headlights flooded into their car.

"He must be crazy," Frank said.

He drove faster, but the truck drove faster, too.

"He's going to get us killed," Donna said.

"I'll pull over and let him pass," Frank said.

He pulled to the side of the road and parked his car, but the truck parked right behind him. The glare of the headlights made it impossible to see the driver.

"Should I go talk to him?" Frank said.

"Don't," Donna said. "He might be dangerous."

Frank thought Donna was right. He waited for about a minute, then said, "I'll just drive off real quick. He won't expect it. Then he won't be able to catch us."

Frank pulled back onto the road. He put his foot down on the gas, but the truck caught up with him in no time.

"He must be out of his mind," Frank said.

He drove even faster, faster than he ever had. The road wasn't safe to drive on like this. At every curve, he almost lost control. But the truck was still behind them. He was sure it would run them off the road.

"Look!" Donna said, pointing to a sign on the side of the road. It said they were only a few miles from town. "We just have to get there. Then we'll find someone to help us."

Frank drove as fast as he could. No matter how fast he went, the truck kept up with him. Finally, the woods ended, and he saw lights up ahead. It was a gas station.

Frank pulled into the gas station and parked the car. He knew the truck was still behind them, and they'd have to make a run for it to get inside before the driver got to them. But when they got out of the car, the truck was gone. They looked for its headlights, but didn't see anything except the empty road. When they listened for its engine, all they heard was wind.

TRUE TALES

All of these stories are based on events that actually happened.

Mike and Ted shared a room at the college. One night, Mike woke up. He felt like the room had gotten very cold somehow. As his eyes got used to the darkness, he thought he saw a dark figure in the corner of the room. At first, he couldn't say a word, but finally, he was able to whisper to Ted just loud enough to wake him.

Ted woke up. When he looked at the corner of the room, he froze in terror.

The dark figure looked like a young man about their age. But he wore old-fashioned clothes. He didn't say anything. He just stared at them for a few minutes. Then, suddenly, he disappeared.

Mike didn't sleep well the rest of the night. Neither did Ted. The next morning, though, they told each other they had probably just imagined it. Their eyes must have played tricks on them in the dark.

But the next night, the same thing happened. They woke up to find the room much colder than it should have been. And they saw the same young man standing in the corner, staring at them.

They told the school what was happening. No one really believed them, but they switched them to a different room anyway. Two other young men took their room.

Those other young men saw the same thing, though. Some people started to say the room was haunted by the ghost of a student who was murdered there. Soon, no students would sleep there.

So one of the teachers at the college said he would sleep there. He didn't believe in ghosts, and said he would prove there was nothing to be afraid of.

After spending one night in the room, though, he changed his mind. He told everyone who worked at the college that the stories were true. He'd woken up in the middle of the night, just like the students. The room was cold, and in the corner, he saw a young man in old-fashioned clothes staring at him.

The college decided the best thing to do was close off the room. They boarded up the windows and locked up the door.

This all happened many years ago. To this day, the college still keeps the room closed, and no one has ever spent the night there since.

UNDER THE BED

A husband and wife were on vacation together. They checked into their hotel room in the morning, and went out for the rest of the day. When they got back to the room, though, they noticed a strange smell.

The smell was so bad that they had trouble sleeping. They complained to the hotel manager, but he said there was nothing he could so. All the other rooms were taken. So, they tried to ignore the smell.

But each night it got worse and worse. By the third night, they couldn't sleep at all. They told the manager to come to the room himself and see how bad the smell was.

When the manager smelled the room for himself, he said it would need to be cleaned right away. He didn't know what was causing the smell, but he hoped that would help.

The cleaning people vacuumed and scrubbed all around the room, but the smell didn't go away. Then, they lifted up the bed to clean beneath it.

What they saw made all of them scream.

A rotting, dead body.

CLICK CLICK

Rose, Brenda, and Jan were sisters. They lived in a small house with their mother. She always got home late from work. Most nights, they spent time together in the kitchen until she got home. The only way in and out of the kitchen was through a door to the hallway. There was a lot of crime in their town, so they always kept that door locked until their mother got home.

One night, they were waiting for her when they noticed the door handle twist, like someone was trying to open it from the other side. "Mama?", Rose asked, but there was no reply.

"Let's pretend we're having a big party," Jan said. "If we make a lot of noise maybe we can scare them away."

The three sisters talked real loud and clanged pots and pans together, but whoever was on the other side of the door kept trying to get in.

Then, the door handle stopped twisting. For a moment, the sisters thought the person on the other side must have left.

That's when they heard a different sound. *Click-click. Click-click.*

They all realized what it was. Now the person in the hallway was switching the light on and off, on and off, for no reason. It seemed like whoever it was wanted to scare them.

Jan called the police, but the police in their town usually took a long time to show up. They were always busy with other crimes. The sisters' mother wouldn't be home for another two hours. They couldn't wait that long. If the person in the hallway was crazy, they might try to break through the door. It wasn't a very sturdy door. They might be able to if they tried hard enough.

The sisters tried to come up with a plan. As they were talking, the noise continued. *Click-click. Click-click.*

Finally, they decided to each grab the sharpest knife they could find and run into the hallway. They thought if they all ran in there at once, they could scare away whoever was on the other side of the door.

Each sister lined up by the hallway door. Brenda was the oldest, so she went first.

She opened the door and ran into the hall. All the sisters screamed and held their knives up high to make them look even scarier.

The light was off. It was almost pitch black in the hallway. But each sister could see the dark shape of a man running up to the attic stairs.

They didn't follow him. Instead, they waited outside for the police. When they finally showed up, one of the officers went inside to check the house.

When he came back, he said he didn't find anyone. There was just one clue: an open window, up by the attic.

FOOTSTEPS

My mother's family didn't have a lot of money when she was growing up. They all lived together in a small house. Everyone had to take turns sleeping in the attic. It was dark and scary up there. The person who lived in the house before them had killed himself up in the attic. But there wasn't enough space in the other rooms. On this night it was my grandmother's turn.

She had been asleep for about an hour when one of my aunts called up to her. "Mama, are you okay?" she asked.

"Yes, everything is fine," my grandmother called back. "Why?"

"I heard footsteps," my aunt said. "I thought you couldn't get to sleep."

"I've been asleep this whole time," my grandmother said. "You must have been hearing things."

It was an old house. They always heard a lot of strange noises like that.

My grandmother started to go back to sleep. She almost dozed off when something else woke her: the sound of footsteps on the other side of the attic. They were heavy, like a man's. They kept getting closer to her, slowly but surely.

My grandmother didn't know what to do. If she tried to run, there was no way she would escape in time.

The footsteps got closer, until they stopped right in front of her. It was too dark in the attic for her to see anything.

After a moment, she heard the sound of a man laughing. The sound came from the spot where the footsteps stopped. The man laughed and laughed and didn't seem to stop.

My grandmother was terrified. There was no chance she could get away now. She was a very religious woman, so the only thing she could think to do was pray. It seemed like she prayed for hours.

Finally, the laughter stopped. She heard some more footsteps, then a creaking noise. After a few moments, she found the courage to turn on the light.

There was no one there, but my grandmother did see something else that scared her. The floor of the attic was always pretty dusty. In the dust, she saw a large set of footprints.

THE MAN IN THE WINDOW

Mary lived with her mother and sisters in the city. One night, she couldn't sleep. There was a big storm keeping her awake.

As she lay there in bed, she thought she heard the doorbell ring. But it was so loud with all the rain and lightning that she couldn't be sure. Besides, it was the middle of the night. No one would be ringing the doorbell in the middle of the night during a storm.

A few seconds later, though, she heard it again. This time, she was sure it was real.

"Mom will get the door," she told herself. "I'll just stay here."

But the doorbell rang a third time, and still, no one answered it.

So, Mary crept out of bed and walked down the hallway to the door. She was very scared, and wanted to wake up one her sisters to come with her, but decided not to. She was the youngest, and she didn't want them making fun of her. They might laugh at her for being scared of a doorbell.

She stopped at the top of the stairs. The front door was down at the bottom. It had one small window on it, shaped like a diamond.

Looking in through the window was an old man. He looked up at Mary, and pressed the doorbell again.

Mary stood there, staring at the man in the window. He kept looking at her, and he kept ringing the doorbell, but the storm was so loud, and no one else would wake up.

She stood at the top of the steps like that for minutes. Finally, she snapped out of it, and ran down the hallway to wake up her mother.

"Mom," she said, "There's a man at the door. He just keeps ringing the doorbell. I don't know what he wants."

Mary and her mother went back to the front door, but when they looked out the window, there was no one in sight. They watched the street for a while, but it was empty. No one would be out in a storm like that.

THE SIDE OF THE ROAD

A husband and wife, Fred and Karen, were driving down a dark mountain road one night. It was a curvy road, and a lot of people got in accidents there.

As they were driving, Karen saw a woman standing on the side of the road. She had a lot of blood on her. Fred drove right past her, though.

"Did you see that?" Karen asked.

"See what?" Fred replied.

"That woman back there."

"I didn't see anyone," he said.

It was very dark and Karen was very tired, but she knew what she saw. She told Fred to turn around and drive back. The woman looked like she was hurt and needed help.

When they got back to the spot there was no woman there. Karen and Fred parked on the side of the road and got out to look for her.

There was a steep hill next to the road. Karen saw a wrecked car at the bottom of it. She and Fred climbed down to get a better look.

"They must have driven off the road," Karen said.

When they looked in the car, the woman Karen had seen was in the driver's seat. She was dead.

Next to her was a small boy. He didn't say a word, but he was still alive.

Fred and Karen called 911 and told them what they found. When the doctors got there, they said it looked like the boy hadn't eaten in days. He would have died in only a few hours if they hadn't found him.

"I guess the woman must have found a way to crawl out and get up to the road," Karen said. "She must have been trying to get help. Maybe she went back to the car after she saw us to check on her boy."

"That's impossible," a doctor told her. "This woman has been dead for at least three days."

BIBLIOGRAPHY

Angeles, Bob. "Shitai and O'lwa." *Urban Legends Online.* UrbanLegendsOnline.com, 20 Feb. 2010. Web. 1 Aug. 2017.

Brunvard, Jan Harold. *The Encyclopedia of Urban Legends.* ABC-CLIO, LLC, 2012.

Chung, Nicole. "5 Korean Urban Legends That'll Keep You Up At Night." *Odyssey.* Odyssey Media Group, Inc., 27 Mar. 2017. Web. 10 Jun. 2017.

Dockrey Young, Richard and Judy. *The Scary Story Reader.* August House, Inc., 1993.

Farnsworth, Cheri. *Haunted Hudson Valley.* Stackpole Books, 2010.

"Highway 50 Phantom." *Unsolved Mysteries.* NBC. 21 Feb. 1997.

Jones, Louis C. *Things That Go Bump in the Night.* Syracuse University Press, 1983.

Kensler, Marian. "The Farmer Vanishes." *Strange Horizons.* Strange Horizons, 12 May 2008. Web. 10 Jun. 2017.

Leach, Maria. *The Thing at the Foot of the Bed and Other Scary Tales.* The World Publishing Company, Inc., 1959.

Mikkelson, David. "The Body Under the Bed." *Snopes.* Snopes.com, 13 Jun. 1999. Web. 8 Aug. 2017.

Padron, Garrett. "The Hanging Tree." *Urban Legends Online.* UrbanLegendsOnline.com, 19 Feb. 2010. Web. 1 Aug. 2017.

Ryall, Julian. "Tokyo homeless woman lived in stranger's cupboard for a year." *The Telegraph.* Telegraph Media Group Limited, 30 May 2008. Web. 7 May 2017.

Schexnaydre, Paul. "Fort Mountain Haunting." *Urban Legends Online.* UrbandLegendsOnline.com, 19 Feb. 2010. Web. 5 Aug. 2017.

Wikipedia contributors. "Black dog (ghost)." Wikipedia, The Free Encyclopedia. Wikipedia, The Free Encyclopedia, 21 Jul. 2017. Web. 9 Sep. 2017.

Wikipedia contributors. "Shadow person." Wikipedia, The Free Encyclopedia. Wikipedia, The Free Encyclopedia, 26 Aug. 2017. Web. 9 Sep. 2017.

NOTES

Followed Home

As far as I can tell, this story originally comes from Texas. In some variants, the man following the girl is the ghost of a slave. Scary stories often reflect the buried fears of a culture. The slave's ghost is a reminder of America's troubled past. However, not all versions of the story contain this element. Instead, the ghost can stand in for anything.

Vanished

I first heard this story as a child. The magazine reported it as true, but after much research, I've found that most versions of this story are inspired by Ambrose Bierce's "The Difficulty of Crossing a Field." This telling is a combination of several different variants.

The Shadow Man

The shadow man is often seen by people suffering from sleep paralysis. Most agree it's a hallucination, but some have claimed that friends and family members will also see the shadow man too.

The New Bride

Scary stories gives us the chance to learn about other cultures. This story is a Korean urban legend. All across the world, there are many scary stories featuring vengeful spirits.

The Backseat

Although this story has been retold in many different places, this version is based on the telling in the classic *The Thing at the Foot of the Bed*. It updates the anxieties of the haunted house trope by placing the haunting in a vehicle instead.

The Dare

This story is loosely based on an urban legend that grew in popularity when a photo supposedly showing a ghost started to circulate throughout the internet. There are many popular scary stories in which a dare goes wrong. Not all of them include pictures.

The Black Dog

People have reported forerunners of death in the form of black dogs for centuries. This telling is based on no particular version. Sometimes the dog is menacing, while other times it simply follows the character without harming them.

The Haunted Treasure

Growing up in New York's Hudson Valley region, I am very familiar with the tale of Captain Kidd and his buried treasure. This story is based on an account in *Things That Go Bump in the Night*, a classic collection of New York State ghost lore by Louis C. Jones.

The Prison

This is another tale in which a dare goes wrong. I included this additional variant because it is loosely based on a number of allegedly "true" accounts, although I've been unable to track down any valid sources to support such claims.

Milk Bottles

Scary stories are a lot like jokes sometimes: they end on a line or image that completely changes everything you heard before. This telling is based on a version of this story which appeared in *The Thing at the Foot of the Bed*, by Maria Leach.

The Picture

The internet has allowed certain urban legends to gain greater popularity. This story appears a lot on forums and websites dedicated to scary stories. In earlier versions, the character must develop her film, but in the digital age, she can check her pictures as soon as she gets home. This telling is based on no particular version.

The Guest

Although this story is frequently reported as being true, it's taken on the status of an internet urban legend. Sometimes people will post videos claiming they are the actual surveillance tapes, but these claims are false. Still, it's interesting that the internet has allowed people to add images and videos to enhance urban legends.

The Man in the Road

This is another urban legend that has been around for decades. The internet has made it popular, with many people sharing the tale as a cautionary warning.

The Bag

As is often the case with urban legends, when I first heard this story, a family member said it was a true account from a friend of a friend. For years, I assumed that it was. Only later did I learn it's actually a fairly popular urban legend. It bears a striking resemblance to cautionary stories like "The Hook."

The Message

The urban legend of "The Roommate's Death" has been popular for decades. Many folklorists believe it first gained prominence on college campuses. Students would share it, trying to scare one another. Some versions, like this one, move the setting from a college dorm to an apartment complex. These basic urban legends usually feature young characters who are on setting out on their own. They speak to the fears that people have as they set off into the world without their parents to protect them.

The Date

"The Boyfriend's Death" is a classic urban legend. This telling is based on no particular version. Although the tale typically ends with the young woman waking up and a police officer telling her to walk away from the car and not look back (which, of course, she does), versions like this one offer a more simplified telling.

Scratching Sounds

This is yet another version of "The Roommate's Death." While the earlier version in this collection generates fear with its shocking ending, this version creates tension before the ending, making it worthy of its own entry.

Something Wrong

Although this story isn't medically accurate, versions of it have circulated throughout the United States for decades. The fear of snakes and insects is already common in many people. The fear of the body being invaded by such pests is often even stronger.

The Elevator

This basic urban legend has grown more popular in the days of the internet. Like many, it highlights the fear young people experience when they live in a big city, surrounded by people they don't know.

The Truck

Scary stories are part of the local folklore of a region. I grew up hearing tales about Clinton Road in nearby West Milford, NJ. As a teenager and college student, I took many trips there myself. Although I never experienced anything frightening myself, many report stories similar to the one told here. Some believe the truck to be spectral in nature, while others suspect it belongs to angry locals trying to scare teenagers off the road.

The Haunted Room

This story is based on actual events that occurred at the United States Military Academy at West Point. Cadets woke up in their room each night and reported seeing the ghost of an old soldier. When others—including officers—stayed in the room, they saw the same. It remains boarded up to this day.

Under the Bed

The tale of the body under the hotel bed is such a well-known urban legend that most people assume it's false. However, this has occurred before.

Click Click

My mother fueled my love of scary stories early by telling me about her own frightening experiences growing up in a dangerous neighborhood. Although names and character details have changed, this story happened to her when she was a child.

The Attic

My mother told me this story actually happened to my grandmother. I've changed certain details to simplify the telling, and added others (namely the footprints) to enhance its impact, but otherwise, I've reported it as she told it.

The Man in the Window

Yet another story from my mother's childhood. Sometimes, the simpler a tale is, the more frightening it is. The image of a man peering in through the window has always frightened me.

The Side of the Road

I first heard this story on an episode of *Unsolved Mysteries*, another favorite among many who grew up loving scary stories. The woman in the segment is convinced what she saw was real. Almost no details have been changed, except for character names.

ABOUT THE AUTHOR

Joe Oliveto is a freelance writer whose work has appeared in such major digital publications as The Huffington Post, Cracked, Time, Thrillist, and many more. In his spare time, he still enjoys reading as many scary stories as he can. To share your story, send him an email at Joseph.Oliveto@gmail.com.

Facebook
Instagram

Made in the USA
Middletown, DE
15 January 2024

47873322R00038